Aesop's Fables

6-in-1 Series
Awesome Aesop's Fables

ISBN: 978-93-5049-400-4

Printed in 2018

© Shree Book Centre

Published by

Shree Book Centre

8, Kakad Industrial Estate, S. Keer Marg, off L. J. Road
Matunga (west), Mumbai 400 016, India
Tel: +91-22-2437 7516 / 2437 4559 / 2438 0907
Fax: +91-22-2430 9183
Email: sales@shreebookcentre.com
Website: **www.shreebookcentre.com**

Contents

Preface

Aesop was an ancient storyteller who lived in Samos, Greece, around 600 BC. It is believed that he was a slave to a man named Xanthus. He used his cleverness to obtain his freedom, and then he became an advisor to kings.

Aesop narrated simple stories to tell the important truths of life. He was a keen observer of both animals and people. Most of the characters in his stories are animals. Some of the animal characters take on human characteristics; they are personified through speech and emotions. However, the characters retain their animalistic qualities. For instance, the tortoises are slow, the hares are quick, and the tigers eat the deer. The qualities and natural tendencies of animals are used to explain human traits and wisdom.

Even today, Aesop's fables never fail to delight and entertain readers. Each story has a moral to be learnt for life.

The three books in this series comprise 18 of Aesop's most popular fables. Written in simple language and printed in large font, the stories are easy to read and understand. Each story is accompanied by colourful illustrations that make reading a sheer delight for children. The glossary of difficult words at the end of each volume will enhance children's vocabulary. Parents too will enjoy reading these evergreen stories with their children.

The Farmer, His Son, and the Donkey

Once upon a time, there lived a farmer with his son. They had a donkey. One day, the farmer thought, "This donkey is of no use to me now. I better sell it." So, the next morning, the farmer and his son took the donkey to the market.

As it was a hot day, the farmer decided not to sit on the donkey and tire the animal. A few people who saw them started laughing. They said, "Look at the fools! It is too hot to walk. At least one of them can sit on the donkey."

The farmer heard the people talking. It was indeed hot and it didn't make sense for both of them to walk. So, the farmer asked his son to sit on the donkey. His son was quite comfortable now.

The donkey was tottering slowly, with the farmer's son on his back. The farmer was walking behind them. Hardly had they walked a few miles when a few people started staring and jeering at them. "Look at that selfish son!" said one of them.

"He looks so young and energetic, but he is sitting on the donkey, while his old father is walking behind him," said another. The son heard this and felt bad for his father. So, he got down and asked his father to sit on the donkey.

Some distance away, two old women were sitting outside their house. When they saw the farmer riding the donkey and his son walking behind, they remarked, "Look at the father! He sits comfortably on the donkey, while his young son walks behind."

When the farmer heard the old women talking, he thought, "I am being selfish. My son must be tired. It is really cruel of me to make him walk, while I enjoy a comfortable ride on the donkey." So, the farmer made his son too sit on the donkey.

Another mile passed. A few farmers working in the fields saw the farmer and his son riding the donkey. They exclaimed, "Look at these merciless people! They are torturing the poor donkey with so much load."

Hearing this, the farmer and his son were quite annoyed. They immediately got down, lifted the donkey, and started walking.

On their way, they came across a river.

As the farmer and his son were crossing the river, a few children saw them carrying the donkey. The children clapped and heckled. Hearing this, the donkey got frightened and trembled in panic.

The farmer and his son lost their balance and their hold on the animal. When the donkey went hurling down the river, the farmer and his son could only look on helplessly.

The Lion, the Monkey, and the Camel

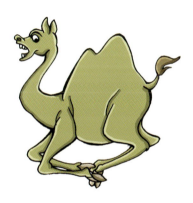

One evening, the animals of the forest were in a festive mood. They were hustling and bustling everywhere, decorating the trees, bushes and caves too. And why not? After all, it was the birthday of their beloved king, the lion.

After the decorations were done, the animals started assembling outside the lion's den. The rabbit brought fresh flowers and the monkey brought sweets. All the animals brought something or the other for their dear king.

"Our king must be here anytime now," said the rabbit. "Hmm, he must be getting ready," said the elephant, nodding his head.

Just then, the king came out of his den, looking very majestic. Next to him stood his minister, the tiger. The lion looked around and was impressed by the decorations.

The lion sat on his throne regally. All the animals cheered for him. They sang songs for him and gave him the gifts they had brought.

The king was overwhelmed with the love and affection of his subjects.

The lion acknowledged the gathering by waving his hand.

Then the tiger said, "With your permission, O King, shall we start the entertainment programme?"

"O sure!" said the lion.

"So, the party begins!" cheered the tiger. All the animals clapped.

First came the monkey. He prostrated before the king. Then, with a sudden jerk, he sprang on a tree and hung upside down from a branch.

Next was the big elephant. He curled his trunk and trumpeted with respect to the king. Then he lifted his front legs and started walking on his hind legs.

The lion and all the other animals were amused.

But the camel standing alone near a bush wondered what the big deal was.

"Why does the king applaud these fools so much?" thought the jealous camel. "I can perform these tricks better than the monkey and the elephant."

The camel jumped in front of the lion with his crooked legs.

The monkey noticed that the lion did not like the camel's vain attitude. He whispered into the camel's ear, urging him to go back to his place.

But the camel did not listen to the monkey. He raised his front legs and tried to walk on his hind legs. Alas, he fell down! Even then, he did not stop. He got up and started singing and dancing. In his excitement, the camel lost his balance and collided with the lion.

The lion, who was seething with anger, yelled at the camel, "This is too much! I can't take it anymore. You are too conceited and adamant." Then the king banished the camel from the forest.

The camel was rightly punished for his jealousy and false pride.

The Fox and the Crane

Long long ago, there lived a fox in a dense forest. He was very cunning. All through the day, he roamed about here and there, mocking passers-by. Seeing them turn red with embarrassment, the fox laughed and jeered at them.

One morning, when the fox was drinking water in a pond, a crane came flying from somewhere and perched next to him.

The fox decided to have some fun. So, he invited the crane for lunch.

The good-natured crane readily accepted the fox's invitation. That afternoon, the crane went to the fox's house for lunch. But he was in for a shock!

The fox knew very well that a crane could not eat from a flat dish.

But, to embarrass the poor bird, he served food in a plate. "Have some soup, dear friend. I have cooked it especially for you. I know how much you love soup," said the cunning fox.

Saying so, the fox began to lap up the soup. The crane looked on helplessly. With his long beak, he tried to sip the soup from the flat dish. But he was unable to do so. Though he was angry, the crane kept quiet.

The crane realized that the fox had made a fool of him. So, he decided to teach him a lesson. Before leaving, the crane invited the fox to his house.

The next day, the fox was at the crane's house.

"Welcome, friend!" said the crane. "I smell something delicious in your kitchen. What did you cook?" asked the fox. "Dear friend. I have cooked your favourite fish," said the crane, as he served food.

When the fox saw the tall, narrow-mouthed jar, he was disappointed.

The aroma of the food made the fox's mouth water. But he was unable to eat from the jar.

With his long beak, the crane finished his food quickly.

The crafty fox could only rub his hands in despair. He kept looking at the food longingly.

The fox then realized that the crane had done this on purpose.

"I understand how hurt others feel when I mock or trick them," thought the fox. He left the crane's house with a heavy heart.

From that day, the fox never mocked or fooled anyone. The clever crane had taught him a lesson—a lesson the fox would never forget.

The Village Mouse
and the City Mouse

Once upon a time, there lived a mouse in a small village. He had made a cosy hut for himself in a green field. The mouse spent the entire day nibbling wheat and corn.

Miles away, in the city, lived his cousin, in a small hole in a stylish house.

One day, the city mouse visited his cousin in the village. "Hello, my brother! We are meeting after a long time!" squeaked the city mouse. "Welcome dear. Nice to see you," said the excited village mouse. They hugged each other.

The village mouse led his cousin into the hut.

After a bath, the mice had some food. Then they went to bed. The city mouse had a nice, peaceful sleep. He woke up fresh the next morning and had a hearty breakfast.

The village mouse took his cousin around the village. He showed him the fields of corn and wheat.

The city mouse was pleased to see so much greenery and scenic beauty all around.

One day, the city mouse said, "It has been more than a month since I came here. I should get back home now. Why don't you plan a trip to the city? Life there is a lot of fun!" "Sure! I shall come next month," promised the village mouse.

The city mouse then took leave of his cousin and went back home.

After about a month, the village mouse visited the city mouse. The city mouse was delighted to see his cousin.

The city mouse took the village mouse around the city. The village mouse was amazed by the hustle and bustle of city life. He was impressed by the tall buildings and frightened by the speeding cars.

The village mouse enjoyed the malls, the movies and the museums. The two cousins returned home late in the evening. "It was a hectic day, but it was wonderful too!" said the village mouse, digging into the delicious dinner of soup and pastries.

Just then, the house was filled with thick smoke that choked the mice. The village mouse coughed and coughed till his throat croaked.

Both of them ran out of the house for fresh air.

As soon as they came out, they found the owner of the house standing there with a thick stick. "Thud! Thud!" he thrashed the mice. Somehow, they managed to escape. It was a horrible experience for the village mouse.

When they returned to the hole, the village mouse gasped, "Is this how you live? Life in the village is not fast and modern, but it is peaceful." The village mouse immediately set out for his village. The city mouse had to accept the truth, although it embarrassed him.

The Deer and His Antlers

Many years ago, there lived a beautiful deer deep inside the forest. The deer was very energetic. He spent the entire day running from one end of the forest to the other. Sometimes, he admired the flowers along the way and sometimes he talked to the birds.

One hot day, the deer was drinking water in a nearby pond. He drank to his full. Just as he was about to leave, something caught his attention. "What's that?" he wondered. It was his reflection.

The deer's antlers looked amazingly beautiful in the clear water of the pond. He could not take his eyes off them. He felt proud of himself. "I must be the most wonderful animal in the world," he thought.

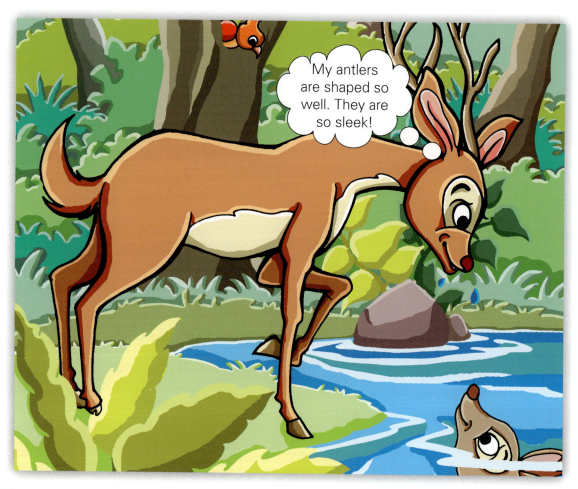

But the very next moment, his eyes fell on his legs.

"Oh no! Are these legs mine? They are so crooked and skinny! I don't believe this," the deer lamented.

"Aargh! With such legs, I must be the ugliest creature in the world," he thought, feeling very sad.

All this while, a tiger was observing the deer from behind the bushes.

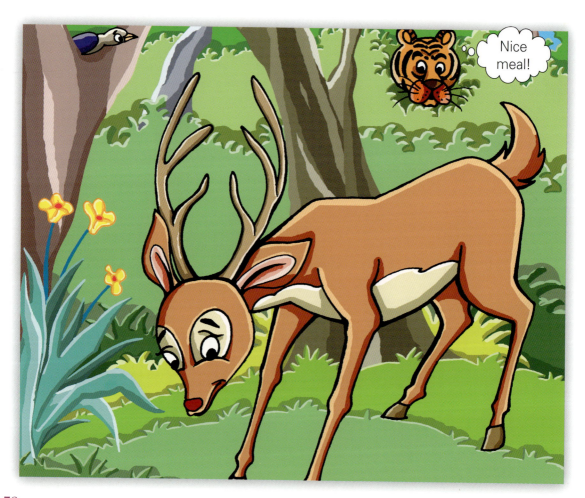

Unaware of the lurking danger, the deer was lost in his thoughts.

Slowly, the tiger crouched close behind the deer. But the clever deer heard the rustling of dry leaves and grass and became alert.

The fierce tiger was about to pounce on him, when the deer took to his heels. Dodging the bushes and rocks, he ran for his life. In a few leaps, he was miles away from the tiger, thanks to his swift legs.

"What a relief! The tiger can't catch up with me," thought the deer.

But he didn't know what danger awaited him. As the deer ran past a leafless tree, his antlers got entangled in one of its branches.

The deer could not move even an inch. He tried hard to free his antlers from the branch, but in vain.

By then, the tiger had caught up with the deer and appeared there.

The tiger would have easily caught the deer, but luckily, the deer managed to free his antlers in the nick of time. He ran away as fast as he could. Once again, his legs had saved him.

The deer's prized possession, his antlers, had landed him in trouble. But his skinny legs had saved him. This taught the deer a valuable lesson not to accept anything at face value.

The Owl and the Grasshopper

It was a winter morning. All the trees and plants in the forest were covered with snow. There had been steady snowfall the previous night and the entire forest appeared white. There was dampness and gloomy silence all around.

The rabbits preferred to stay inside their burrows, the little birds in their nests, and the jackals inside the caves. Not a single animal dared to venture out in the cold. "Don't play in the open today. Better be here, tucked inside your blanket," the mother rabbit told her naughty child.

The owl too was crouched in his cosy home, in the hollow of a huge tree. He didn't feel like stepping out for food too. He curled his wings and fell asleep.

But out in the snow, a grasshopper was enjoying the chillness.

He hopped and jumped around and then perched on the branch of a tree.

The chirping of the grasshopper annoyed the owl who had been sleeping peacefully.

"Who is making so much noise in such calm weather?" he thought.

The owl peeped out of his house and saw the grasshopper. "Eh! What are you doing in this biting cold? Go back home!" snarled the owl.

But the grasshopper was in no mood to be quiet.

For him, the cold weather seemed pleasant. He was more active than ever.

The owl was surprised to see the grasshopper making merry when all the other animals were shivering in the cold.

He called out to the grasshopper again and asked him to keep quiet.

"This may be fun for you, but it is a nuisance to others. Stop making noise and go back home," said the owl.

The bird then curled under his blanket. But the grasshopper did not pay any heed to the owl. "Tra … la … la … la … la …," he continued, louder than before. The owl became furious.

He was already annoyed by the damp winter. And now, the grasshopper was adding to his woes. He once again warned the grasshopper.

But the foolish creature did not stop singing.

The angry owl swooped upon him. He swiftly caught the grasshopper in his sharp claws. And that was it!

In an instant, the owl swallowed the grasshopper.

"This is for ignoring my request," the owl said, smiling. Then he flew back to his cosy bed and pulled the blanket over him.

"Zzzzzz," snored the owl as he slept peacefully. And the forest plunged into silence once again.

Meanings of Difficult Words

The Farmer, His Son and the Donkey

tottering	–	moving unsteadily
jeering	–	making fun of; teasing
energetic	–	full of life; lively
merciless	–	cruel; without any pity
torturing, tormenting	–	causing mental and physical pain

The Lion, the Monkey and the Camel

prostrated	–	lay face down in respect
applaud	–	clap; cheer
seething with anger	–	very angry; bubbling with anger
conceited	–	proud; vain
adamant	–	stubborn
banished	–	sent away from one's own country or land

The Fox and the Crane

mocking	–	ridiculing; teasing
crafty	–	cunning
despair	–	unhappiness
longingly	–	with a deep desire

The Village Mouse and the City Mouse

nibbling	–	pecking; taking small bites
scenic	–	beautiful; charming
hustle and bustle	–	commotion due to many activities
hectic	–	very busy
thrashed	–	beat up badly
embarrassed	–	felt uncomfortable

The Deer and His Antlers

crooked	–	bent; not straight
skinny	–	very thin
lamented	–	mourned; expressed grief

lurking	–	hidden; waiting in hiding
crouched	–	ducked down with knees bent and upper body brought forward, to avoid being seen
in vain	–	without success

The Owl and the Grasshopper

dampness	–	wetness
gloomy	–	dark and sad
burrows	–	underground holes in which animals rest or live
venture	–	try or set out
nuisance	–	bother; inconvenience
heed	–	attention